The Adventures of
David and Goliath

Goliath's Easter Parade

The Adventures of
David and Goliath

Goliath's
Easter Parade

Terrance Dicks

Illustrated by
Valerie Littlewood

Piccadilly Press . London

Text copyright © Terrance Dicks, 1987
Illustrations Copyright © Valerie Littlewood, 1987

Phototypeset by V.I.P. Type Ltd., Milton Keynes, Bucks.
Printed and bound by R. Hartnoll, Ltd.,
Bodmin, Cornwall
for the Publishers, Piccadilly Press Ltd.,
15 Golders Green Crescent, London NW11 8LA, 1987

British Library Cataloguing in Publication Data
Dicks, Terrance
Goliath's Easter Parade.——(Adventures of David and Goliath; 7)
I. Title   II. Littlewood, Valerie   III. Series
823'.914[J]   PZ7

ISBN 0-946826-79-X

Other titles in THE ADVENTURES OF DAVID AND GOLIATH series
GOLIATH AND THE BURIED TREASURE
GOLIATH AND THE DOGNAPPERS
GOLIATH ON HOLIDAY
GOLIATH AT THE DOG SHOW
GOLIATH'S CHRISTMAS

Terrance Dicks is the producer of the BBC TV Classic Serial,
and is one of the most popular children's authors.
He is well known for his novelisations of **Dr Who.**
Piccadilly Press publish his ASK OLIVER series, T.R. BEAR series,
and THE CAMDEN STREET KIDS series.
He lives in the Hampstead area of London.

Valerie Littlewood lives in Lincolnshire.
She has illustrated a wide range of titles for various publishers,
and is an increasingly popular illustrator.

Chapter One

Playgound in Peril

"Close down our adventure playground?" said David in horror. "They can't do that!"

Goliath, David's huge shaggy dog barked in agreement. Or at least he barked as David finished speaking, so it sounded as if he was agreeing.

Mike, one of the young helpers who ran the playground, ruffled the fur on Goliath's head. "I'm afraid they can. The council say they've just got to make some cuts and we've been elected."

David just couldn't believe it. The adventure playground had been part of

1

the fun of the common as long as he could remember.

It wasn't much to look at, just a ramshackle collection of rope-swings and climbing frames and beams and pillars and concrete tunnels and car-tyres and ricketty wooden platforms and petrol-drums painted bright colours – everything you could possibly climb on or through or under or jump off or swing on or bang on.

The fact that it was so shabby and scruffy was part of its attraction. You couldn't really hurt or damage anything – except yourself if you were careless.

There was a big old Nissen hut attached to the playground fitted out with chairs and trestle tables and the cheerful young men and women who ran the place were always arranging events – treasure hunts and

story-reading and painting and craft-work competitions.

"Can't you do anything?" David asked.

Mike shrugged. "Apparently there are charities and trusts that give grants to places like this, but it takes time to make your application and get it accepted. Everyone seems to think we've a good chance of raising money for next year, but it's this year that's the problem. Our funds will have run out by Easter, and that's only a couple of weeks away. It's all been very sudden. We thought we'd got at least six months before any more cuts."

David was thinking hard. "So if you could raise enough cash to keep going this year, next year might be okay?"

"That's right – but we'll never do it in the time."

"Of course we can do it in the time,"

said David determinedly.

"How?"

"I don't know but there must be some way – there always is." David had a bright idea. "I'll have a word with the Residents' Association, they ought to be able to help."

Tugging on Goliath's lead, David hurried away.

*   *   *

The Residents' Association was made up of people who lived in the little cluster of streets around the common. They helped to look after the common itself, and tried to keep an eye on things in the area. They often ran fêtes and jumble sales to raise money for various good causes, and David couldn't think of a better cause than this one.

There was a meeting of the association next evening, and David asked if he could come. The meeting was being held in his front room, so he didn't have far to go.

David explained the problem and the members of the association listened sympathetically.

Miss Gorringer, the President, said, "David's right, we certainly ought to help. The question is how?"

"Can't you have another jumble sale or something?" asked David.

"I don't know if people will stand for yet another one. We need something different," said David's mother. "Something original."

There was a bit of a silence as everyone tried to think of something.

But nobody did.

"We've got to come up with something," said David desperately. "If we don't manage to raise that money by

Easter . . ." He broke off. "That's it, Easter. We'll have an Easter Parade – on the common!"

"How will having a parade raise money?" asked Miss Gorringer.

"Oh, all sorts of ways," said David's dad. "You have a competition for the best costume, the best float, the best anything. Everyone pays an entrance fee, and you try to get someone to donate the prizes free. You can have raffles and things. And then there's sponsorship – you get local firms to give you a donation in return for advertising their shops on the lorries and floats . . ."

There was a lot more discussion, and everyone agreed that this was a brilliant idea.

"Well, we'd better get busy," said David's dad. "Easter's not far away, and there's a lot to do."

Miss Gorringer nodded. "I'll start getting the necessary permissions right away."

"What permissions?" asked David.

"Well, you can't just have a parade whenever and wherever you like, you know. I'll have to get in touch with the police and the council and all sorts of people . . ."

Everyone worked very hard setting up the parade in the weeks that followed.

David and Goliath did their bit by going round all the local shopkeepers and asking for sponsorship. David was helped by the fact that all the local shopkeepers knew Goliath. Unfortunately Goliath was a bit on the greedy side, and he'd got a habit of cadging little treats.

However, for once David was glad

that Goliath had so many friends. The
big dog seemed to be welcome
everywhere, and almost everyone they
asked seemed willing to sponsor the
parade.

Miss Gorringer and David's parents had been busy too, as had the other association members. They'd got sponsorship from banks and estate agents and places like that, and local organisations like the Boy Scouts and the army cadets had agreed to have floats in the parade.

In fact, everything was going well – too well as it turned out.

Then came disaster.

*   *   *

It happened just a few days before Easter.

The Residents' Association were having their final meeting, just to check that everything was under way.

They'd got permission from the police, and there were lots of entrants in the parade. What with entry fees and sponsorship money, it looked as if they'd raise enough to keep the playground open for the rest of the year.

Then Miss Gorringer arrived. She was late and flustered and she was waving a long brown envelope, the kind unpleasant official letters always come in.

"I'm terribly sorry to be late," she gasped. "I've just got this letter from the council. It says we're not allowed to have the parade after all!"

Chapter Two

"Never take no for an answer."

Everyone stared at Miss Gorringer in astonishment.

"I thought we'd settled all that," said David. "You said the police gave their permission ages ago."

Miss Gorringer sat down, fanning herself with the letter.

"So they did – it's the common that's the problem. I wrote to the Town Clerk as well, and he wrote back saying it would have to be approved by the council but he was sure that there wouldn't be any problem. I took that as the go-ahead." She held out the envelope. "Then this came."

David's father took out the letter and read it aloud. "The Town Clerk regrets that owing to the special provisions of the Common Trust it is not possible to give the permission you request. The trust's rules expressly state that no kind of demonstration, procession or parade may be held on the common at any time."

"What's this trust then?" asked David. "Don't the council run the common?"

"Well, they do and they don't," said Miss Gorringer. "I telephoned the Town Clerk and he said this trust has some kind of interest as well. It seemed very complicated. But he said quite definitely that we weren't allowed to have our parade."

David's father sighed. "Well, that's it then. We can't have a parade at all if we can't use the common."

"Hang on a minute," objected David. "We're not just going to give up without a fight, are we?"

"What else can we do?"

"We can find out something about this trust for a start. Maybe we can get them to change their minds."

"How can we? We don't even know who they are," said Miss Gorringer.

"Maybe not," said David. "But we can find out. And I know just the person who can tell us!"

"Who's that?"

"Miss Hollings, my history teacher. She knows everything about the common." David jumped up, "I'll be back as soon as I can. Don't cancel anything, don't say a word to anyone."

David couldn't quite believe he'd made such a speech in front of

everyone, but he was determined.
Goliath's excited tug on the lead
reassured him he'd done the right
thing.

*   *   *

David sat in Miss Hollings's kitchen,
while Goliath romped in the garden
with Scrap, Miss Hollings's Yorkshire
terrier.

She was one of the nicest of David's
teachers, tall and thin and vague and
always caught up in good causes.

The common was a particular interest
of hers, and as David had hoped, she
knew all about the trust.

"There are three of them, David,
descendants of the three families who
originally presented the land to the
council. When they made the gift they
also made some provisos, some rules, so
that the common shouldn't be used for

anything they'd disapprove of. The rule saying no parades must be one of them."

"Well it's a daft rule," said David indignantly.

"Maybe it is," said Miss Hollings, not unsympathetically. "Anyway, the best thing you can do, David, is to go and see the members of the trust and see if you can get them to change their minds. "I've got all their names and addresses

here, I had dealings with them that time someone tried to build on the common. They were very helpful . . ."

She copied the names and addresses from her book onto a piece of paper and handed it to David. "Here you are."

David studied the three names. "Sir John Jeremy, Commander Dillworthy and Lady Jane Martingale." David gulped. "Sound a pretty posh lot, don't they?"

"Don't you be afraid of them," said Miss Hollings firmly. "They're only people just like anyone else. And remember, David, in a good cause, you must never take no for an answer."

*   *   *

David was doing his best to think of Miss Hollings's advice next morning as he set off to tackle the first member of the trust.

Sir John Jeremy was Managing Director of JJ Supermarkets, and apparently their head office was above the big supermarket in the High Street.

David had high hopes of success with Sir John. JJ Supermarkets had agreed to sponsor the parade, so Sir John couldn't really want to have it stopped.

David paused outside the supermarket, wondering what to do about Goliath. Like most food shops the supermarket had a NO DOGS sign and they'd provided dog hooks outside the door.

The trouble was, Goliath hated to be left outside anywhere and always gave a series of long loud mournful howls until David came to collect him. He sounded so pathetic that passers-by often ticked David off for neglecting his dog.

Still, there was nothing else for it. David was just about to tether Goliath to the hook when the most tremendous fuss broke out inside the supermarket – shouts and yells and cries of "Stop him! Stop thief!"

A thuggish-looking young man came clattering down the centre aisle with a group of white-coated assistants chasing after him. He was clutching a blue cloth money-bag under his arm.

Seeing David and Goliath apparently blocking the doorway, he skidded round and ran up the next aisle.

Instinctively David gave chase, Goliath lolloping beside him. Suddenly David had an inspiraton. "Fetch!" he yelled. "Ball, Goliath – fetch."

Goliath gave him a puzzled look, looked at the running man, saw the blue bag and jumped, as David had hoped, to the wrong conclusion – that the blue bag was some kind of ball, and the nice man wanted to play with him.

Barking excitedly, Goliath put on a turn of speed and jumped up at the running man from behind.

The man gave a yell of alarm, swerved wildly and crashed into a stack of baked bean tins, sending cans rolling everywhere.

Goliath jumped on top of him, snatching the blue bag from his hand.

The man scrambled to his feet and disappeared through the open front door in a flash.

One of the assistants came running up.

"I'm afraid the robber got away," said David calmly. "But Goliath's got the money back for you!"

He pointed to Goliath who was standing there with the cloth bag in his mouth, wagging his tail.

"Good dog," said the assistant, reaching for the bag.

Unfortunately Goliath thought it was all part of the game and they had to chase him all over the supermarket to get the money-bag back.

They managed it at last, and the breathless young assistant said, "Sir John, our Managing Director wants a word with you."

"That's fine," said David cheerfully. "As a matter of fact, I want a word with him!"

Sir John Jeremy was exactly what a tycoon ought to be, a big, jolly man smoking an enormous cigar. He thanked David for helping to recover the money, patted Goliath on the head, and then, after David had explained about the parade, dictated a letter on the spot saying he had no objection whatever to the parade going forward.

"I'm sure Commander Dillworthy won't mind either," he boomed. "You may have trouble with Lady Jane, though. As old as the hills and tough as teak. Used to be a suffragette, you know . . ."

Only half listening, David hurried away, clutching his letter. He'd made a good start, he thought. One down and two to go.

Commander Dillworthy didn't sound too bad. But how on earth was he going to tackle Lady Jane . . .

Chapter Three

The Nelson Touch

"I'm sorry but the Commander is not at home," said the fierce looking housekeeper. She gave David and Goliath a suspicious look and prepared to close the door of the big old house.

"You couldn't tell me when he'll be back, could you?" pleaded David. "It's very urgent."

"I'm afraid I couldn't say. The Commander is boating on the common." In more human tones she added, "Fair crazy about that silly old boat he is. I shouldn't be surprised if he's late for his tea – and his feet wet into the bargain, silly old codger!"

And with that she slammed the door.

Puzzled, David set off for the common. What had she meant, boating? There was a biggish pond on the common, but it wasn't a boating lake . . .

When David got to the edge of the pond he understood.

An enormous model steam-yacht, a good six feet long, was floating in the exact centre of the pond. It was a magnificent affair, completely detailed, with gleaming brass and mahogany everywhere.

Standing by the bank, jabbing furiously at a radio-control was a white-haired blue-eyed old man in a navy-blue duffel coat, welly-boots and a woolly hat.

David went up to him and said politely, "Splendid boat, sir."

"Take a good look at her," said the old man gloomily. "You won't see much more of her, and nor will anyone else."

"Why not?"

"Because the ruddy remote control's broken down, boy, that's why. She's stuck in the middle of the pond and she's sprung a leak." He stared gloomily out at the stranded yacht.

"You are about to see an old man's pride and joy disappear!"

"Mustn't let that happen, must we?" said David cheerfully.

Thankful that it was a mildish spring day he stripped quickly down to his underpants, piling his clothes neatly on the bank.

He plunged into the pond, ignoring the NO SWIMMING notice on the bank.

David wouldn't have thought of disobeying the notice normally. But this was an emergency and despite his small size, David was a strong swimmer.

With Goliath, who loved swimming, paddling along beside him, David swam quickly out to the sinking model yacht.

Reaching the side of the yacht, David trod water, putting one hand on Goliath

and using him as a sort of living life-raft.
With the other hand he slipped the loop
at the end of Goliath's lead over the
model yacht's funnel, then turned and
swam for the shore.

Goliath followed, towing the yacht
behind him.

It was as simple as that.

When they reached the bank, David

helped the old man to pull the boat to the shore where it lay on its side, water pouring from the leaks in its hull.

The old man took off his duffel coat and insisted that David use it as a combined dressing tent and towel.

In a matter of minutes David was both dry and fully dressed again – except that is for his pants, which he wrung dry and stuffed in his pocket. Goliath shook himself, sending spray everywhere.

The old man got David to help him load the boat on to its special mini-trailer and said determinedly, "Now you're coming back home with me my lad, and you're going to eat the biggest and best high tea you've ever had in your life. And when you've finished there'll be a handy sum in cash for you – you've got salvage rights in that vessel, you know."

As they trundled the trailer along the path David said, "I really don't want any money, sir, thank you very much. But you could do me an enormous favour . . ."

"Name it, young man. You deserve it. Talk about the Nelson touch! 'Lose not an instant', that's the Navy's motto, and you certainly didn't. Straight in, splash! So, what's it to be?"

"Well," said David. He paused. "Er, you are Commander Dillworthy, aren't you?"

"I most certainly am!"

"Well, it's about this Easter Parade, Commander . . ."

An hour or so later, David and Goliath were on their way home after a tea that was every bit as good as had been promised.

In his pocket David had a second letter authorising the parade. What's more, he felt the third letter was as good as his already, since the Commander had promised to speak to Lady Jane for him as well.

"I wouldn't try tackling her yourself," the old man had said confidentially. "Lady Jane doesn't like boys or dogs. Doesn't like anyone very much as far as I can make out. Lives in that big old house you know, on the hill overlooking the common. Thinks it's still her back garden!" The Commander shook his head. "Wonderful old girl, mind you. Must be eighty or ninety now, and still sharp as a needle. Frightens the life out of me. Used to be a suffragette, you know, years ago . . ."

Commander Dillworthy had promised to telephone Lady Jane, explain about the Easter Parade, tell her that he and Sir John Jeremy were in favour and get her to send a letter of consent like theirs. "You'll have all three letters in plenty of time. Must have all three you know, all the trust have got to agree."

Grateful for the old man's help, David had thankfully given up the idea of tackling Lady Jane. She sounded a real old dragon . . .

*   *   *

Time went by and plans for the parade began to take shape. David had given Miss Gorringer the two letters of consent, and she'd passed them on to the Town Clerk with a promise that the third was on the way, so that took care of that problem.

The adventure playground was naturally being used as Parade Headquarters and all the lorries that would be carrying floats had been parked behind it. Teams of workers from all the organisations taking part were hard at work on their floats.

The plan was for the parade to set out from the adventure playground, follow a circular route through all the streets round the common, return to the common and make a final circuit and then stop for the closing ceremonies and the judging.

It was the very night before the parade that things went wrong. The parade was going to be on Easter Monday. On Easter Sunday the Parade Committee, which consisted of the Residents' Association, the adventure playground staff and a few other helpers as well, was having its final meeting in the big playground hut.

It was a fine spring evening, and David and Goliath were playing outside the hut.

A huge gleaming Rolls Royce limousine turned in at the entrance to the common and drove slowly along the road round the edge until it reached the playground.

The car stopped, and a white-haired old chauffeur in tunic, cap and leggings got stiffly out, a big parchment envelope in his hand. He gave it to David, who was the only one in sight, got back into the car and drove slowly away.

On the front of the envelope was written: "To the Parade Committee. From Lady Jane Martingale. By Hand."

David took the letter to the door of the hut.

"Miss Gorringer," called David.

She looked up. "What is it, David? We're all very busy."

"I think it's the letter from Lady Jane, the third letter of consent."

"Just open it to be sure, will you, David, then you can put it in my in-tray and I'll send it to the council. She's left it a bit late, hasn't she?"

Standing in the doorway of the hut, David opened the envelope and drew out the single sheet of stiff white paper that was inside.

There was a crest on the top of the sheet of paper and a message written in neat, almost copperplate writing.

The message said, "Lady Jane Martingale presents her compliments to the committee and regrets that she cannot see her way to agreeing with her trust colleagues on the matter of the proposed Easter Parade.

"She therefore declines to give her consent.

"The committee will appreciate that since all three members of the trust must give consent for permission to be valid, the parade cannot now take place."

David read the notice at least three times before the meaning of the stiff formal language sank in.

She was saying no!

She was saying they couldn't have their parade.

"Is it from her, David?" called Miss Gorringer. "Is everything all right?"

David looked at the busy group around the table, thinking of all the hours of work they'd put in, his own parents among them.

He looked at the lorries in the car park with the teams adding final touches.

He looked at the adventure playground itself, doomed without the money the Easter Parade would bring in.

He took a very deep breath and then he called steadily. "Everything's fine, Miss Gorringer. She says we can go ahead!"

Chapter Four

The Crunch

Relieved, Miss Gorringer turned back to her meeting.

Stuffing the letter in his pocket, David turned and hurried away. He couldn't, *wouldn't*, disappoint all the people who'd worked so hard, just for the sake of one old woman's selfish whim.

Two out of three of the trust had consented and that would have to do. But what had he done? He'd never lied like that before.

David's mind went back to his tea with Commander Dillworthy. The old sailor had told him a story about Nelson,

England's great naval hero.

It seemed that at the beginning of some sea-battle Nelson had been ordered to retreat because enemy ships had appeared and he was badly outnumbered.

Nelson, who had lost one eye in some earlier battle, had put his telescope to his blind eye and said, "I see no ships!"

Then he'd gone on to take on the enemy and win.

"Well, I see no letter," said David fiercely to himself. "Once the Easter Parade's over she can kick up all the fuss she likes!"

*　　　*　　　*

Despite his bold words, David had a sleepless night. He kept tossing and turning, so much that Goliath who slept beside and sometimes on his bed didn't get any sleep, and whined in protest.

Would he be sent to prison or something, wondered David.

He was unusually silent over breakfast next morning, but his parents were too busy and too excited to notice.

In a bustle of last-minute plans and decisions, they made their way to the adventure playground where the parade was assembling.

All the decorated lorries were lined up in order and they made a splendid sight.

The staff of JJ Supermarkets had turned their lorry into a supermarket counter filled with giant cans and packets, with members of staff dressed as cans of beans and pieces of cheese and apples and pears.

The bank staff were coins and notes in a giant till and the cadets had what looked like a full sized cannon.

The operatic society had a little stage on their lorry with an opera going full blast.

The Youth Club had a giant juke box and a life-like Elvis Presley.

All the way down the line there were amusing or amazing scenes.

David thought to himself, "Whatever happens, it's worth it. The parade will be a smash!"

Two black cars drove in at the entrance to the common and drove slowly towards them.

One was the big Rolls Royce limousine David had seen the day before.

The other was a police car. David looked twice at both and his stomach started to churn.

"What do they think they're doing?" grumbled David's dad. "We won't be able to get the parade out unless they move!"

The two cars drew up by the hut.

Looking very embarrassed, Commander Dillworthy and Sir John Jeremy got out of the Rolls Royce. A uniformed inspector got out of the police car.

A third passenger sat unmoving in the back seat of the Rolls, a tall, thin-faced, white-haired old lady with a beaky, aristocratic nose and a little turban-like fur hat on her head.

The window slid smoothly down, but she didn't speak.

Sir John Jeremy spotted David and said apologetically, "Lady Jane saw the parade assembling from her windows this morning, and sent for us – and the police."

Commander Dillworthy said, "She says she sent a letter yesterday, refusing her consent."

"We never saw it," said David's father.

"I saw it," said David quietly. "I decided not to tell anyone." He waited to be dragged away by the police.

"Why on earth didn't you pass on the letter?" asked Commander Dillworthy.

David gulped. He tried twice to speak and then finally his voice came, squeaky at first then a bit firmer.

"I thought her refusal was stupid and selfish," said David. "She didn't deserve to be taken notice of."

Lady Jane's head went up and she spoke in a clear high-pitched voice, with no trace of the tremor of old age. "Your opinion is unimportant, boy. Rules are rules. The law is the law and must be obeyed."

"What about stupid, unfair rules?"

"They should be changed – but until then, they must be obeyed."

Suddenly, David remembered something. He went closer to the car.

"Didn't you once use to be a suffragette, Lady Jane?"

"If you are going to be impertinent, boy . . ."

"Please listen," said David desperately. "If I've got it right, the suffragettes were protesting against the rule that women couldn't have the vote – just because they were women. That was the law in those days – and the suffragettes chained themselves to railings and caused all kinds of fuss in protest."

Even after so many years there was anger in Lady Jane's voice. "Denying women the vote was stupid and unfair."

"Exactly," said David. "*And stupid, unfair rules ought to be changed!*" He paused. "You could change this one now."

There was a long, long pause.

Then Lady Jane said, "I withdraw my opposition. The parade can begin. I am sorry to have inconvenienced you, Inspector, you may return to the station."

The window slid up and Lady Jane was driven away.

The police inspector, who hadn't said a word, sighed wearily, got back in his car and followed her.

David's father too heaved a sigh of relief. "Right then, let's get this show on the road!"

As David had predicted, the Easter Parade was a smash.

Cheering crowds lined every inch of the route and they raised enough money, what with sponsorship and collections, to keep the adventure playground going for the rest of this year and a bit of next.

Late that afternoon when the parade had dispersed – the Youth Club juke box won first prize – the committee sat in the adventure playground hut discussing the day.

Miss Gorringer patted David on the back. "And a lot of it was due to you, young man!"

"Goliath helped too," said David.

He turned as the Rolls Royce limousine drew up outside the hut.

The silent chauffeur got out, came into the hut, gave David a large parchment envelope and got back in the car and drove away.

"Oh dear," said Miss Gorringer worriedly. "I hope she hasn't changed her mind and decided to have us all arrested after all!"

"You'd better open the envelope, dear," said David's mother. "It seems to be for you!"

David opened the envelope, drew out the single sheet of paper and read the message out loud.

"Lady Jane Martingale presents her compliments to the Easter Parade Committee, and is happy to formalise her consent to the afternoon's proceedings.

"She begs that the committee will accept the enclosed donation to what she now believes to be a most worthy cause."

David fished inside the envelope and took out the cheque. It was made out for a hundred pounds!

"Well, there's the aristocracy for you," said David's dad. "You've got to admit, the old girl's got style." He ruffled David's hair. "Still, I reckon you were lucky to get away with it, my lad. She

51

might very well have had you locked up in the dungeons of the Tower of London. It worked this time but don't try it again. Still, how did you manage it?"

David grinned, and patted Goliath.

"Nothing to it, dad," he said cheerfully. "Just call it the David and Goliath touch!"